3 YEARS

SOUVIK BOSU ROY

Contents

Acknowledgements

I want to thank to my late mother **Kanika Basu Roy** for teaching me not to give up on anything in any situation until the almighty takes you up, my late grandmother **Sandhya Bosu Roy** without whom I'll be an uneducated shit, **Archita Das** who made me write, **Avik Ghosh** and **Avradeep Das** who stood there with me no matter what the situation is. And also thanks to to **Arindam Pramanik, Rohini Sarkar, Ashmit Gupta, Ashmita Sarkar, Ranajay Saha, Indrani Mukherjee, Shreya Panja, Ankita Bhowmik, Anishes Chakraborty, Sangram Das, Ratnadwip Sarkar** and everyone else who has given their opinions and blessings to support me and inspire me to write this book.

1

Its **3** years from the past. No, I'm not a time traveler. I just suddenly bumped into some memories down the lane. People says what we think before sleeping comes in our dreams. Is it true? Maybe it is. Maybe not. Let's forget it.

So, get back to the point.

It was 2021. A life where I had time to breath freely. A year that changed everything. A year that could have ended in a different way.

14ᵗʰ June, 2021

Hey, it's my 21ˢᵗ birthday.

From now on, I'm an adult. I can make my decisions on my own. I can do whatever I want. I can even marry whomever I want. I can drink. I can smoke. Whatever the f*ck I want to do, I can do. This is what everyone thinks of.

But for me, it was like now I'm an adult who can't give any excuse like a kid. I need to think twice with all the probabilities and decide what's better for me and my loved ones. I can't do anything that could hurt my loved ones; I have to be careful about that. I need a settled career to make mine and my family's future better as much as I can. I have to work hard rather than blaming on my destiny or fate. I have to be responsible as an adult and drinking and smoking isn't a thing as show off my luxury anymore, it's more like a temporary painkiller now.

Although, there was a party in my house to celebrate my 21ˢᵗ birthday. Some of the neighbors were invited and obviously my friends were there but someone else was invited. Ankhi. She was my best friend from Facebook. I know facebook friends can't be best friends under normal circumstances as per the majority in our Indian society. We have heard many things but if we were the persons to give any value to those manmade thoughts, she won't suppose to come today at my 21st birthday celebration which is also held at my house.

But that day, Ankhi didn't come.

2

The birthday which was going to be the best I thought, went as the worst birthday ever. What a start to my adulthood journey? Maybe the people were right about Facebook friendships. Maybe I expected too much or maybe she had some sort of problems to come at my place. She had tried to call me too but why? What if she's not well? Should I go to her house? Am I over thinking about her? Nurturing these thoughts in my dumb shit head, I don't know when but I fell asleep.

She was in her promised black saree, black bangles, black bindi and black earrings. A flower bouquet in her hand full of white and yellow roses furnished with blue orchids around the flowers. A packet in her hand where some gifts were sniffing out from the packet. She lived around Jadavpur (south Kolkata) and I live in Baranagar (North Kolkata). It was one and a half hour to reach my house from her house. She was not so comfortable with the train routes and in bus, she feels Nausea. So, she booked a cab. She was near Tala Bridge.

It was **10.10** P.M., Suddenly a truck took a wrong turn and hit her cab and smashed it badly. Local people came, police came to rescue them but what they found is two dead bodies with blood all over their bodies, they're not even identifiable. The flowers she brought for me were bloody red; her black saree was drowning in fresh blood.

Maybe I was the reason. Maybe if she didn't come for my birthday, it won't have happened. Maybe, I'm the murderer of her. I was crying and sweating heavily. My throats got dry, no sound was coming from my mouth, I'm trying to speak out, trying to shout out, trying to breath for a second but I can't.

Suddenly, Baba came to my room and he woke me up and gave me some water. He was looking clueless or rather to say, his face was frightened seeing my actions. It took me few minutes to understand that I was having a bad dream and having sleep paralysis again.

I checked my phone and got to see her 5 missed calls and text messages asking sorry for not coming at yesterday night's party. I don't know why but I couldn't resist myself and started crying and praying that may this nightmare never turns into reality.

I called her back and said,

Me: Are you safe, Ankhi? Are you well? Are you hurt? You don't have to come to my place. I can't risk your life due to my expectations. Please take care of yourself.

Ankhi: What? Wtf? Are you well? I never risked my life for anyone. And what does it mean by your expectations? I thought, you will be angry on me for not coming at your birthday, you won't talk to me, you will block me and will believe that people were right about our friendship and from that fear, I was saying sorry because I broke the promise of coming at your birthday.

Me: Nothing much! I was....I was.....

Ankhi: Wait a second! Did you have the same nightmare again? Please for god's sake say No, you hadn't!

Me: Yes, I had the same nightmare, I told you before.

3

Ankhi: Have you consulted about this with Dr. Sarkar? You can't be like this. You will be a psycho if you stay like this. Bikram, that was an accident and that has passed 3 years already.

You had nothing to do about that. It wasn't in your hands.

Me: Yes, I had gone to Dr. Sarkar 2 days back. He advised me not to be stressed over anything; Whatever, I'm now okay after talking to you. Now I need to get fresh and eat something. I'm having loose motions too! Tata!

Ankhi: Aren't you behaving strange today? Or is it only to me for yesterday's thing? Look, my grandmother wasn't well and maa called me and asked me to get back to home immediately. I called you right at the moment but maybe you were busy there and that's completely natural for anyone on their birthdays.

Me: No Ankhi, that's not the thing. You don't have to give explanations to me at least. It's just I'm not feeling quite well, just need to get shower. I will text you after that. Tata!

Ankhi: Okay. Your wish. Text me whenever you feel free. We need to talk over your nightmare thing. And please don't ignore this. It's serious. Tata!

I cut the call immediately.

Baba: Baban, what did the doctor said? Don't hide anything from me. I may not be your real father or I may not have any child but for me you're my own son and I think we share a bond that you can share these things with me. I can do nothing but can give you some suggestions.

Me: (taking a long breath) Dr. Sarkar told me, I'm suffering from Parasomnia (which refers to Nightmare disorder). If I get stressed over anything, if I get anxiety, if my sleep schedule gets disrupted, I'll get these nightmares again. And if this continues for few more months then I need to admit in the hospital and get psychiatric treatment as a psychopath.

Baba: Okay. I got it but you have to stop thinking the same thing again and again, stop making you feel guilty for that accident. It was in their destiny, that's why it happened. You're a good son. They are surely proud of their son.

Me: Sumit, what can I do? Do all of you think, I think about that deliberately? No, I don't. It comes to my mind often when I see any moment of that night is repeating and I starts over thinking about that, the unthinkable probabilities hit my frightened brain. You know? Yesterday, I got Ankhi's missed call at 10.10 P.M., she texted me before leaving her house to reach ours' but after that missed call, I couldn't reach her on call and then while over thinking about this I fell asleep and I don't know anything thereafter.

Baba: Were you drunk again?

Me: A little bit! Not much. Wait! See Sumit, yesterday I was drunk too. And you guys think I do these over thinking just baselessly.

Baba: No one said that, Baban. Would you like to eat some Luchi, Alur dam and also the Nolen gurer rosogolla? Get fresh quickly; I'm waiting for you in the dining. (He hugged me and kissed on my forehead and went to the kitchen)

4

I got fresh and ate some luchis, alur dam and my favourite Nolen Gurer Rosogollas.

I had a fear to tell the real thing to Ankhi. I don't know how she would react. I shouldn't have lied to her about this.

Ankhi is caling me! Oh Shit! Why did I post these depressed thoughts yesterday on my WhastApp status.

I picked up the phone in fear of a loud noise beating me over the phone.

Me: Hello, is your breakfast done? What did you ate?

Ankhi: Listen, I'm not in a mood to discuss these things. Tell me what the truth is right now!

Me: What? What truth? I haven't lied to you about anything.

Ankhi: You did. I knew you'll be denying on this but I have to know the real truth.

Me: Please cool down. Firstly, let me know about what lie you're talking.

Ankhi: Your nightmares. What is the real reason behind that? You told me that your parents died on your birthday night. They were driving and getting your birthday cake, gifts and other stuffs and were hit by a truck and you were sleeping when they tried to call you. That's what I learnt from you.

Me: And that's what is true! What else do you want to listen?

Ankhi: You know this too Bikram that this was never a truth. Me and Sumit uncle has gone to the doctor few days back when I got to know your parents died in your childhood when you were a 5 years old child and you also had a.....

Me: Can we not talk about her? And this is why I have never called this dumb man as 'Baba'. He doesn't deserve that.

Ankhi: Firstly, accept that no one does for any other's children what he had done for you guys and secondly, why shouldn't we talk about her? And if you don't tell me this right now, we would be two unknown persons for the rest of our lives. I can't bear liars.

Me: Okay, done! Now, drink some water first. But don't tell this to anyone like what Sumit did. Promise me!

Ankhi: But why? Do you have the fear of getting judged for this? Okay, first tell me your truth. Then I will tell you some of my experiences.

Me: Yes, you heard right about our parents. They died in a car accident too. But the nightmare I get every day is of something else.

It was **3** years ago as you know. It was Sneha's birthday.

Ankhi: Sneha? I didn't know that you had any girl in your life except me.

Me: Sneha was my one and only sister, 2 year younger than me. It was her 16th birthday. She was a cute extrovert girl who likes to celebrate small things, happy with her life, singing and dancing every time but....

(Tears were dropping my eyes and making a shape on my chins)

Ankhi: Okay! Okay! Cool down! Can we meet somewhere at around 4 P.M.? I think talking in face to face will be quite more nice than over a phone call.

Me: Maidan? I don't need many people around us, that's why.

Ankhi: Okay done. Please don't be late. I'll be leaving after lying to maa.

Me: Sure! I'll be at Maidan Metro Gate-2. Tata!

Ankhi: Bye and don't fight with uncle. Otherwise, I will beat you up.

5

Evening of 15th June, 2022

It's 3.30 P.M. I'm in the metro thinking about how to tell all that actually happened. I'm over thinking again "How she's going to react after listening all these. She will surely judge me. She will never talk to me or she will slap me with all the force she has."

I reached at Maidan Metro Station Gate-2 a little bit early. She is surely on her way. I bought a cigarette to settle my brain a little more to have the will to confess the truths.

4.05 P.M.

Ankhi: Oii, Sorry for letting you waiting for me. I got late answering all the questions from the test paper maa gave me before getting out of the home.

Me: It's okay! It's just 5 minutes late; even I don't count it as late. So, we should walk now as you have to get back to your home quick, right?

Ankhi: (looking at my eyes, my shaky hands) Yes, let's go! Do you want to have some food or water? It's my treat today.

Me: No, no, I'm good. Let's go. (In same shaky nervous voice)

I know she got the fact that I'm massively nervous and frightened. She held my hand and started walking towards Maidan ground.

We reached at Maidan ground, one of the most beautiful places in Kolkata, one of the favorite places for couples, for photo shoot, horse riding, for sports too with a majestic view of Victoria Memorial beside. You can find nothing but a peaceful place where you can talk peacefully without too much noise.

She held her head on my shoulder and now the phase for which I was literally praying to the almighty to take me up has arrived.

Ankhi: So, Bikram, can we talk now? Or do you need more time to speak out? It's already 4.30 P.M.

Me: No, I'm okay. So listen, whatever you are hearing now, please keep it secret, please. (Taking her hand in mine)

Ankhi: Okay promise but please speak out the thing now.

Me: So it was **3** years ago. My sister's 16th birthday. We had planned a grand celebration for her as on her last birthday, she got sick and we couldn't celebrate her success in her board exam too. She had passed with 76% marks in her boards.

Ankhi: Oh! That's great. She is a good student then.

Me: She was. (Staring towards the top of the Victoria memorial). She is a victim of **'Cerebral palsy'** from her early childhood. We have consulted about her with various doctors but all the doctors did was a lot of tests and said that medical science can do only the treatment, treatment will help her but this can't be cured and in future she might get more affected due to this disorder. She can't walk properly; her motions were involuntary with exaggerated reflexes. As per medical science, there were both the possibilities of surviving a year or lifelong. I took every bit of her, literally everything. I did never oversight her. For her, I was her baba and maa, not anyone else. But even though, I can't save her, I just did let her die with all the pain I could give to her. (Crying my heart out)

Ankhi: Hey, you tried more than enough. You said, the doctors said years before that her survival can't be assured and maybe now she can rest wherever she is without that pain she was suffering through. You're not responsible for that, Bikram.

Me: You will be blaming me after listening the complete story. So, we had planned the celebration of her birthday from 6 months before her birthday. I and Sumit had planned a lot of things together to make them happen. A big panda themed birthday cake in her favorite chocolate flavor, a room full of balloons, full of her favorite tulips and did arrange her favorite foods, all her friends did come to the party. She was so happy and blushing like she was already in the heaven. All these years, we just wanted to see that little girl's smile. The birthday cake got cut, music started, gifts came. Then, while the people were having their food, Sumit told me that we were short of ice creams. So, I decided to bring those and it was already 10 P.M.

I drove my car to the best ice cream shop in our area; literally I was that much happy that day that I can do anything. I bought the ice creams and a special one for my little princess. While getting back to the home, I met some of my old friends. They were drinking as usual. I was out of my mind that I have to go back to home with those ice creams melting in my car. I got some of drinks. While bidding them bye, I noticed Sumit has called me 10 times. It was not usual that he calls me more than twice. I tried to call him back but can't reach. I kept the phone in the car and tried to drive as fast as I could. Reaching the gate of our house, I saw people were gathered at a place. Some of her friends were passing me like horrified and clueless.

I ran towards the jam and I saw...

Ankhi: What?

Me: Sneha was lying in the lap of Sumit who was looking at her like a numb. I was not crying, I was just looking to her face, that little happy face which never let me drop a tear. I got closer to her. Sumit noticed me and asked,

Sumit: You are drunk? Seriously? Do you even know, I had tried how much to contact you when she was dying. Maybe you were not on this planet.

I didn't answer anything, not a single word came out from my mouth.

Sumit told me that few minutes after I gone to buy the ice creams, Sneha felt dizziness in her head and she fell down from her wheel chair, they tried to put some water on her face, called the doctor and Sumit tried to call me to bring my car ASAP and take her to the nearest hospital but he couldn't reach me and by the time, Sneha took her last breadth, the doctor came after a minute she died and declared that she was no more. From that day, I never drove my car, never drunk a little before yesterday night because I was in full of joy expecting you would come.

Tears rolled out from Ankhi's eyes. She hugged me and kept crying.

Me: Now, you should have understand, why I feel myself guilty for this, why I say I'm the only responsible for her death. I know Karma will fire me back and I'm ready for that but for god's sake please don't tell this to anyone, please. Everyone took their finger on me and that's completely reasonable to them but I can't turn the time backwards. Everyone judges me over this, everyone thinks that I didn't like my sister and I deliberately did that. They said that my reason to go out from there was not to bring the ice creams, I gone to drink and have some fun with my fellows. Ankhi, please trust me, I had no intentions to do that to her who was the only reason of my happiness, I loved her more than anything and anyone.

Ankhi: Okay! Stop crying first. I know you and I trust you. You did everything to make her happy and she used to smile only because of you, Bikram. Everyone has their destiny, maybe it was in Sneha's destiny. You can't do anything to it. And from the next time, never lie to me over anything, I'm never going to judge you but I can't bear liars. Just think like the almighty has returned your little princess in as me. It's all destinies. Oh, by the way, do you remember, I told you in the morning that I also have something to confess to you? You do fear that people will judge you over things, right? So if how much judged I got, you will cut yourself off, I bet.

Me: (wiping my tears) I don't understand. What do you mean by that?

Ankhi gave me a slight fake smile and looked at setting sun like something very bad had happened to her in the past.

Ankhi was looking to my eyes like she is going to tell me something with which she's not so comfortable. She took a deep breath and started her story.

Ankhi: It was 2015, **3** years before Sneha's collapse, I was 14 years old then. At that time, I was in 9th standard and was not used to talk with people often. There was a boy in the 10th standard. Rittik. He was a cute tall handsome boy, his eyes were charming, used to play football, his singing was too much of obsession to listen but he was an extrovert unlike me and I don't know why but I can't bear that.

Me: So, let me guess it right, you fell in love with him, right?

Ankhi: Yes, I did. I introduced myself to him during Christmas party of our college group where we sang and danced together like mad men, drunk a little bit, it was my first time drink, so I was like "No, I'm okay to be the dumbass, boring girl, I don't want this to be cool" but then we all know that we all have a friend whom we can't put down. So, while doing all the crazy stuffs, I felt uneasy, dizziness. I went to the bathroom and put some water on my face, started vomiting which continued till the end of the party. Sima, my best friend came to rescue me from that black hole I was into. Then while getting out of the pub, Rittik asked me if he could drive both of us to our homes. We agreed as we were not in the state to travel alone in the night. It was 30 minutes from the pub to reach Sima's house and 45 minutes from mine. He first dropped Sima at her house and then was going to drop me. I was not in me to be very honest with you and I don't know whatever we did but when I opened my eyes, I was lying on my bed. I thought of him being so generous and responsible that he didn't take the advantage of being with a drunk girl alone in his car but after the winter vacation when we went to the school, I got heard some shits about me. It was hovering all around the school that I and Rittik had sex that day after the Christmas party. And you know who had spread this shit?

Me: Rittik?

Ankhi: To be honest, I thought the same at that moment and I couldn't find him around the school for at least a month thereafter. Later on, I came to know that I had a traitor with me all the time. It was Sima, my best friend not Rittik. She told everyone that we had gone to a hotel near to her house after dropping her and we were denying to let her in Rittik's car as we didn't want anyone to disturb us.

Me: And what about Rittik? He didn't spoke out a single word about this? Or did he want to it to get spread as you were surely the most beautiful girl, he met. Mfs!

Ankhi: No, he didn't come to the school after the spreading of that rumor and left the school to save his career as the teachers were also informed about this shit. They called our parents but only my parents attended that parent's teacher meeting where my parents were badly insulted and they portrayed me as a whore. I couldn't prove anything as he wasn't there to clarify the issue. I got beaten up returning home, named like which I can't even tell anyone, Baba started to drop me at the school and pick me up from the school. I was like a criminal to them, a burden that they didn't want to take anymore, and a witch who was putting down the image of the family. I was used to hear Slangs and curses instead of Good Mornings & Good Nights. They tried to arrange my marriage, so that they can be free from me. In India, we all know how fast a rumor spreads, isn't it? It took 1 week to spread this rumor all over our area. People used to comment dirty about me while passing, taunt me, cursed me and everything they could possibly do. I was used to be a girl who cries on almost everything, blames own destiny, complains to the almighty but trust me all these were happening at a huge scale that I started to accept the reality, I trusted in me that I know

I was right, so whatever the people are saying, it's their perspective, their views, their opinions, I shouldn't care about those and focus on myself. I passed my Higher Secondary exam with 90% marks and topped in our school while in the 10ᵗʰ boards I roughly had 52% during that worst phase of my life. I don't know whether your success can remove all the stains on you but it did for me. Everyone in the school praised my success, my parents spread the news of their girl's success all over the area, and everyone greeted me. Baba bought me a new mobile phone due to my results. I was new to the social Medias as I was never allowed to do such things. I created my facebook account and after couple of months, I got a message from somebody. It was Rittik, the coward, selfish guy who ran away even after knowing that I loved him and I will be in the worst problem and my career could possibly get ruined. He texted me sorry for all that happened and told that he has shifted to Hyderabad due to his father's job and he misses the time we spent, the vibes we had shared together and he wants to come to meet me in Kolkata during the Durga Puja.

Me: So, what did you do? Did you meet him? Do you still love him?

Ankhi: Have you lost your mind, Bikram? I instantly blocked him and deleted the chat. I don't want to see his fucking face.

Ankhi was growling into anger and tears were making a shape on her cute chins. I held her close to me, gave her a tight hug and sit for few minutes holding her hands. We both stared at the setting sun. She smiled like my little princess looking at my reactions when my shirt got drained by the dropped shit of a crow. We got up from Maidan ground and left to get my shirt clean first and then to get the famous Mango Lassi at Esplanade beside the K. C. Das outlet. Then she booked a cab and bid me good bye for the day. Her cab drove away from the range of my sight and I stood there for like 15 minutes thinking all she said, all she has experienced, and how much lucky I'm to have her by my side. Even though, we are still best friends, nothing much but it's better to have a best friend like her rather than having a toxic relationship.

I took my metro blushing in my own world and got down at Dum Dum Metro Station. Suddenly, I got a mail.
Me: Whattttttt!?
(Started crying)

Me: Whattttttt!?

All the people there at the Dum Dum Metro Station were looking at me like I just murdered someone. I was be like "hey, what can I do, the mail literally shocked me". It was the mail I was waiting from so long. It was a mail from University of Heidelberg, Germany approving my admission. I didn't know how to react at that moment. It was a dream comes true for me. I called Ankhi to inform about this breaking news I have.

Me: Hello, Ankhi! Have you reached home?

Ankhi: Yes! I was just going call you. Have you reached?

Me: I've reached my dream, Ankhi.

Ankhi: What? I don't understand.

Me: Do you remember, I've told you that I had applied for PhD in University of Heidelberg, Germany? They mailed me their acceptance towards it just a few minutes ago.

Ankhi stayed silent for a minute and said,

Ankhi: Wow! That's great news. I'm proud of you my boy. When're you going by the way?

Me: I have some formalities ahead of the admission, so I need to be there by the 20th of June. It all depends on my visa now.

Ankhi: Oh! That means you have no time to celebrate now. Good, Good. Now go home and call me after having the dinner, we will need to make the list of TODO's for you before going to the country of Hitler. Tata.

Me: Are you upset over it? I don't get the excitement in you what I have expected from you. I think you're thinking something deeply, don't you?

Ankhi: No, I'm okay, Bikram. Why should I be upset over your success? I'm happy for you. It's just the other things hovering in my head.

Me: What?

Ankhi: Nothing. Leave it. Those are silly thoughts. Go home now.

Ankhi cuts the call.

Was I right? Did the news really made Ankhi upset? But it's my dream from being a high school student. I can't risk my career anymore and I'll also come here during the vacations. I love her but I don't even know whether she loves me or she just likes me as a friend. Should I leave it for love or should I choose my career? I'm thinking like a teenager who doesn't' have any ambition, dream or anything like that. I have to go there.

I returned home with a pot of sweets for Sumit and the kids of my neighborhood. For the first time in my life, I hugged Sumit and he heard "Baba" from my mouth for the first time in all these years he has taken care of us, fed us and did more than everything own parents do. The tears in his eyes shown me how much happy he is and how much thirsty he was to hear this 'Baba' word from me.

He made my favorite biryani for the dinner. I told him about the whole situation. He suggested me to pursue my dream and nothing else. According to the lines he told me were "Listen Baban, You don't know or rather say you both haven't confessed about what you do feel for each other, right? So, you both don't owe each other anything. If you value your career over your relationship. Then nobody is going to tell you that you were selfish, you just seen your side and not her. Even if you're in the confessed relationship, I would told you what I'm telling now because if she loves you and you do feel the same, then these obstacles can't break your bonding. Yes, you both might feel sometimes that it will not work due to the distance but you both have to deal with it. Giving up on your partner because of some temporary obstacles you're facing isn't the sign of love. So go to live your dream and be a successful man. I'm proud of you, Baban.

Even though, for the moment, I thought baba's words were correct but later on, I started over thinking on it again. That night, I didn't get any call or text from Ankhi. I was assuming the reason. And due to that stress and pressure, the nightmare, I dreamt again.

The next morning, I woke up with a bad headache at around 1 P.M. in the noon. Opening my eyes, I saw Ankhi beside me. For first, I thought, I'm dreaming again but then baba came with my favorite coffee and made me realize that it isn't a dream.

Ankhi was smiling and I saw a bunch of letters in his hand. I got up and eagerly asked her,

Me: Are these letters? Are they for me? What's inside?

Ankhi: Hey mad man, shut up and sit. Why should I tell you? Are you my boyfriend or what?

Me: I could be if you wanted....I mean, I had this nightmare last night. (I tried to pretend that I have cracked a funny joke even after knowing that it was lame)

Ankhi: Shut up and listen, I will read the letters but you have to promise me that whatever I'm reading right now will not affect any of your decisions or your life.

Me: Okay, I promise, anything will not harm the future of mine.

Ankhi: Okay, so be quiet and don't ask any question before I finish reading it.

Me: Okay. Now start.

Ankhi started to read the letters but listening to it, I don't know how these happened but......

8

Ankhi started reading her letter.

Hey You,

It was 18th September, 2021. I met you for the first time after a year only on the social media. You walked into my life and damn, you made a mark. At first, you were just a friend that I genuinely enjoyed spending time with. We had similar tastes, interests and values. You were there when I needed help with homework and stuck by me through mental breakdowns, moments of weakness and even heartbreak – from others, and from you.

I've never met anybody like you. You're genuine, smart, caring and, well, you're able to handle me, which I applaud you for. You're there for me and that's what made me put all my trust in you. I'm able to open up to you knowing you won't judge me or spill to anyone. You give me advice and support me. You hold my hand when I need someone to keep me up. You believe in me.

When I began falling for you, I was good at ignoring the feelings at first for the sake of our friendship. But, our friendship kept getting stronger by the day and so did my feelings. I knew that what I was feeling was forbidden. I knew that acting on those feelings was not an option. I was falling for my best friend – somebody I couldn't have in that romantic way. I didn't want to risk losing a friend or making the situation weird. The last thing I ever wanted was for us to lose the relationship we had because that was more important to me than anything else in the world.

But, the time finally came – I had to be honest with you for my own sanity. Once I told you how I felt and you said you didn't feel the same, my heart shattered. It hurt, a lot. I was prepared for that, but it still stung. I convinced myself I could get past the heartache. I figured that having you in my life as my friend was better than not having you at all. I thought I could just push my feelings aside and pretend to be okay, no matter how hard it was going to be.

To be honest, it was rough. It still is rough at times.

I'm not going to lie. It's hard hanging out like we always used to with you knowing how I feel about you, along with everything that's happened between us. It's difficult acting like I'm 100 percent okay, like I'm over you and like having a close relationship doesn't bother me. But, I'm happy to keep pretending that it's all okay to keep things the same.

If you were to ask me now where I think we stand, I would say we're not friends anymore. We're more than friends. We are way past *just friends* and you know it. We aren't together, though, and I am completely fine with that, I really am. I definitely know that I care about you a whole freaking lot, and I hope you feel the same.

People probably call me crazy for staying this close to you. But, I don't care. You're my best friend and that tops everything. We need each other in our lives to keep things interesting. I normally don't make promises, but I will make one promise to you: You're my best friend and, as such, I will always be there for you. I will continue to support you, help you, comfort you and be there when you need me for whatever reason, even if another girl breaks your heart. I'll be there for you. Why would anybody dare to hurt you? *How* could anybody hurt you? I'm hoping you'll be there for me too, for whatever I need. That's the way things are meant to be.

Who knows, maybe one day it'll happen. Maybe one day, after toning down this whirlwind of emotions and getting past this awful timing, the universe will bring us together. Maybe one day, you'll feel for me like I feel for you, and when that day comes, we'll take it as it goes. I'm in no rush to get to that point. I'm not hoping or wishing for it to happen. I don't need that to happen. I just need you.

I'll miss you like crazy over the summer or anytime we're apart, really. It's going to suck. But, I'm also so excited to start a new adventure with you when you will return on your summer break.

Sincerely,

Your best friend

Ankhi smiled with tears in her eyes and folded the letters again. Tears dropped from my eyes too.

I started to think again on my departure to my dream.

We hugged each other for a minute or two. Then Ankhi put her letters in her bag again and told me,

Ankhi: You're going to Germany, not out of the world. So go and return as a successful man, my champ. You don't have to think about us. We'll be still like we are now. I love you and that's why I want to take care of your dreams too. It shouldn't be only for men always, women can adjust too if they truly love a person.

20th June, 2022

I left Kolkata, Ankhi and Baba from Netaji Subhash Chandra Bose International Airport at 3.20 A.M. in the morning to first reach Hamad International Airport (Doha) and from there a second flight to Frankfurt Airport, Germany. It was a 14 and a half hour flight journey. Then, from Frankfurt Airport to Mannheim, Hauptbahnhof via train and then again a train from Hauptbahnhof to Heidelberg, Hauptbahnhof.

It's a new journey of life starting in between the clouds. We never know what's coming in our lives. It seems like a second life after a traumatizing past life. I called baba and Ankhi after reaching the University Campus. I did complete the remaining formalities and got my admissions. Now it rest time after a long hectic day.

Good night!

9

Everything was going very smoothly. I topped my 1st year examination and did well in the second year too at the University of Heidelberg.

Ankhi got a job in the US a year ago. Baba was left alone in India. Both of us visited him during the Durga Pujas and every time when we went back his face looked like he was mourning on someone's funeral. I wanted to take him to Germany but he was a lover of his beloved nation and I decided to respect his decision and love for his country.

4th October, 2024

It's Maha Saptami. I just returned home on yesterday night. Baba had arranged a king's dinner for me. Ankhi didn't come this year. She told me that she was overloaded with her work there in the US. Although, I & baba spent a great Durga Puja, mostly spent our time at our colony's puja. It's not anymore pandal hopping, hanging out with friends, now it's a time for some refreshment, leisure and some father-son time for us. We went to the bhasan of maa durga. Everyone in Kolkata feels both the heavy air of sadness for maa durga's return and the craziness for the last day of Durga puja. While returning home, I got a WhatsApp text from Ankhi telling me that she wants to tell me something very urgent. I returned home along with baba and called her.

Me: Hey, What's up? Subho Bijoya! How was your day?

Ankhi: Subho Bijoya! Please don't ask me that dumb question. How would you expect I'm having a great day or a great week while sitting in this US, not in Kolkata?

Me: Sorry miss. I just returned home from our colony's bhasan. I couldn't receive your call due to the loud music and dhak's sound. Was it that much important call that you called five times knowing that I won't be able to take the call at the bhasan?

Ankhi: Yes, aren't you drunk right now? It's dashami.

Me: No, I told you so many times before that I have quit drinking and smoking. Why don't you trust me, Ankhi?

Ankhi: So, I'm returning to India tomorrow.

Me: Oh, that's great. Let's make the plans then. Wait, I need to tell baba about your arrival.

Ankhi: Wait and sit for few minutes and listen to me first.

Me: Anything serious?

Ankhi: Yes and whatever I'm telling you, please don't tell uncle, not a single word of it. Promise?

I was getting anxious now. Does she don't want our relationship to be continued or if she has met a new boy who is better than me or if her family pressuring her for marriage?

Ankhi: Do you remember, in the last month you fell down due to a sort of dizziness?

(We had gone to the doctor and had done some tests including MRI of your brain.)

Me: Yes, have the results come? How're the results? Have you consulted with Dr. Belly?

Ankhi: Yes, the results came early in the morning and I had gone to Dr. Belly in the afternoon but...

(Ankhi started to cry and then a minute of silence on the phone)

Me: Hey, why're you crying? What happened? I'm fine.

Ankhi resisted her tears and said,

Ankhi: It seems normal to you but not to the doctors, as per the doctor you had a tumor in your brain, did you know that?

Me: Yes but I was given the treatment for that with the form of medicines and that was from when I was in the 7th standard. And the doctor had told me that it will be fine by the time and the medicines. So, is it still there?

Ankhi: And you didn't tell me that for one single time, great! And you call me your everything. What a liar you are.

Me: Hey, why are you getting so angry on this? I didn't tell you because we all thought that it's fine now.

Ankhi: Ohh, wow! Then you need to know that you are now a patient of **Medulloblastomas**.

Me:What's that? It's more like a Chinese food than a disease LOL.

I started laughing and she was getting angrier.

Ankhi: Moron, It's a type of brain cancer which developed from your brain tumor. It started in the lower back part of the brain where your tumor was and tends to spread through the spinal fluid and after some time it develops as cancer.

Everything around me suddenly stopped. I was numb.

After a silence of minutes I said,

Me: Ankhi, so how many days of my survival left?

Ankhi: A month or two.

She was crying like she has already lost me.

Me: Should I tell this to baba? He should be prepared to arrange my funeral.

Ankhi: Stop! Please stop. Don't tell him anything now. I'll tell him everything about this tomorrow when I'll be there beside him.

Me: Is there nothing we can do, Ankhi? I don't want to die, Ankhi. I want to live my dreams; it's the last year of my college. I had dreamt so much. Baba will be a living dead if I die. I had so many plans. Our holiday plans, our long awaited Maldives trip, our hangouts, our Dura Puja night outs, our Maidan gossips, our evening tea, I had promised uncle aunty that I'll never make you cry but I'm doing it too. I'm sure that this is the karma for me for the death of Sneha. It's her curse for sure.

What if.......

I fell down and lost my sense that day. The doctor came and told that it was due to excessive mental pressure I was taking but I couldn't tell baba what was my mental pressure is all about. Ankhi will be coming in an hour.

Ankhi came and took baba to his room and told everything. I knew baba will be in deep black hole and that's what it is.

16ᵗʰ June, 2025

3 years ago on this day, Ankhi had confessed her love to me sitting beside me and this is the day when she was still sitting beside me but the situations are changed. It was my last chemotherapy which lasted for 6 months and its 10.10 P.M., I'm writing this diary for the last time before burning into ashes. I hope, Ankhi will get a better person that I was who will treat her in the best way possible, Baba's food business will grow more and more. Life is so unfair but also fair sometimes. Maybe, I was a good person that's why almighty is taking me up in the sky to take care of Sneha, my princess. Just kidding though. It was a beautiful rollercoaster journey throughout these 25 years of life with everything in it. Nothing more. Now it's time for me resting in peace. In the next life, I'll complete the bucket list I have left. Tata.

I wrote a letter for baba & Ankhi.

Ankhi & Baba,

After my departure, I want you to know that I've lived a full and good life and you were the reason it went good.

I had the opportunity to pursue my dream, experience both the bad phase when Sneha gone and the best phase when I got Ankhi, I was the most fortunate son to have a father like you.

If I've wronged you in any way, I am sorry.

We are multitudes, and a lesser version of me did not treat you as well as I could have.

In addition to the rainbow of emotions I've experienced, of particular note are the immense gratitude and happiness I felt during my time here.

Please don't despair over my death. Just recall a song and smile on my funeral "Kabhi Alvida Na Kehna"

While I might not have been ready to leave, I was glad to have lived.

Let that be of solace to you I'm leaving behind.

I love you,

Baban/ Bikram

3 different years, 3 different tragedies, 3 different personalities